On A Wild Adventure

On A Wild Adventure

Story by Kudzai Pasirayi

Copyright © 2016 Kudzai Pasirayi
All rights reserved.

The author asserts their moral right under the Copyright, Designs and Patents Act, 1988, to be identified as the author of this work.
All Rights reserved. No part of this publication may be reproduced, copied, stored in a retrieval system, or transmitted, in any form or by any means, without the prior written
consent of the copyright holder, nor be otherwise circulated in any form of binding or
cover other than that in which it is published and without a similar condition being imposed on the subsequent purchaser.

Author:	Kudzai Pasirayi
Title :	On A Wild Adventure
Edition	1
Publisher:	Createspace Independent Publishing
ISBN-13:	978-1539455745
ISBN-10:	1539455742

Edited and Published in the United Kingdom
Cover Design © DreamHunter
Illustrations © Eugene Zhitnikov
Printed by CreateSpace Independent Publishing Platform

All rights reserved.
Copyright © 2016 K.Generation Productions

"The bottle of Milk has slipped into the lake and sunk into the unknown. How am I ever going to find it again?"

One night....

In the centre of Village of Maddern, a little rabbit named Ralphie laid restlessly on his bed as he thought of the lost bottle of Milk his mother Eva had sent him to buy from Mr Patterson's store.

He looked out of his window deep in thought for some time until he finally fell asleep.

The night was still young and the bright sparkling stars shined across the Village of Maddern while the frogs croaked quietly down the lake. The full moon looked kind and peaceful that evening.

As the night got darker, winds started to blow furiously as the rain poured down filling the lakes and rivers across the Village. Trees were blown in all directions, leaving the ground covered in damp leaves. Mama Eva woke up to check on her little sleeping rabbit. She closed his curtains and turned off the lights .

Ralphie slept peacefully and entered Dreamland, which His Uncle Walter had always told him about. It was a place where anything was possible, like the idea of going on a safari trip, where Ralphie had always wanted to go with his friends. The Dreamland was full of possibilities and a place of fun adventures.

As the cheeky rabbit slept, he suddenly saw himself near a waterfall with his friends Rico, Olivia and Woodie. As they were playing in the waters, the sun shone brightly and the colourful birds flew past them, singing cheerfully. Whilst he was dreaming, Ralphie was standing near the water shores when he saw something falling from the skies that looked like a bottle of milk glisten in the sun. It was so wonderful to watch. He met his friends Rico, Woodie and Olivia. They jumped blissfully in joy as they had found it.

As the dream went on, Ralphie ran cheerful to his mother and she thanked him for finding the lost bottle of milk. What a fun adventure it had been in Dreamland.

When morning came, Mama Eva said, "Ralphie get up, today I need you to go and call your Aunty Rosa."

However, all Ralphie could think of as he got out of his bed, was how the dream felt so real. It had been the most marvellous dream he had during that long night. Dreamland was indeed full of possibilities. Ralphie was not hungry that morning. He got up, opened the door and went straight outside to do what he had been instructed to by Mama Eva. He walked to Aunty Rosa's place, but he still could not stop thinking about the dream from last night.

Was it possible for him to ever find the lost bottle of Milk?

Where would he actually go to search for it?

But in his dream, Ralphie had seen himself holding a bottle of milk but in reality, he had just lost it the day he was sent to Mr Pattison's store at the lake with his friends.

Unfortunately, the bottle of milk vanished mysteriously into the unknown and there was no way of getting it back.

Ralphie had wanted to prove to Mama Eva that he would find it no matter what. But she warned him, as it was tremendously dangerous for her little rabbit to go on a search for a bottle of milk. Like always, Ralphie was determined to find it. That day was the day when he hoped he would find it. He would use his dream to guide him, remember what Uncle Walter had said,

"Anything is possible in Dreamland"

It was a beautiful sunny day and the birds sang magically. Flowers blossomed beautifully by the roadside in the Village of Maddern. Although it had rained the night before, the sun still shone brightly across the beautiful village. He decided to head in the direction of the lake to complete his secret search. Once again, he heard his name being called.

"Ralphie, Ralphie"

"Wait up," exclaimed Rico.

"Who is it?" "Who else could it be?" Ralphie thought to himself.

Ralphie turned around to see his friends Rico, Olivia and Woodie who had been running beside the bushes. "Hi Ralphie, why are you heading to the lake by yourself?" asked Woodie. His friends could see that Ralphie was still in his thoughts, as he kept quiet when Woodie asked him.

"Ralphie, Ralphie"

"What are you thinking about?" asked Olivia, the pretty, girl rabbit.

"I had a dream last night in which I had found the bottle of milk that we lost the other day. My uncle Walter said anything is possible in Dreamland. I really wanted to prove to my mother I can find the lost bottle of milk. It must be down the waterfall, which leads to the lake. Do you guys want to go on a secret search with me? No one must know that we are going to the lake by ourselves." said Ralphie

"Yes, Yes, I want to go Ralphie. I'd love to go on a search. Like your dream, maybe we might find the lost bottle of milk," fearlessly shouted Rico.

"What if we get lost, Ralphie, who will rescue us?

What will our parents do?" Woodie looked really concerned.

"Ohhh don't start to worry Woodie, we can never get lost, it's only the waterfalls. Come along Olivia, let's go with Ralphie." Rico said trying to comfort worried Woodie.

"So are you all saying yes to a secret fun adventure? "Let's go and find the bottle of milk!", exclaimed Ralphie.

"Yes, yes, let's go!" shouted Olivia

At once, the rabbits looked around; they found no one watching them as they took the path which led to the lake leading to the waterfall. It was a long walk. The rabbits spent a good deal of time walking into the forest that led to the waterfall. None of the wild animals, which Woodie knew to habit in the forest ever harmed them. They often came close to insects and seemed to be moving in groups' .The yellow striped butterflies flew delightfully. Ralphie and Woodie jumped trying to catch one but they failed. The birds sat on the branches nearby and sang their sweetest songs.

Eventually the little rabbits got to the edges of the lake, where they saw a bottle near the water shores.

They all jumped in joy thinking they had found the bottle of milk.

Woodie decided to take a step further and he realised it was just a bottle with what seemed like a map as it had arrows pointing north. Ralphie quickly grabbed it from him.

"I think we should follow this map. I want to prove I can find the bottle of milk," shouted Ralphie

"No, no Ralphie, I don't think it is a good idea, we might get lost," said Worried Woodie.

"Well, we still have time to find it. Let's follow the map, who knows, we might find the bottle of milk," exclaimed Rico.

"Oh look guys, there is an empty canoe. We can get on it and follow the map. What a fun adventure this will be," shouted Ralphie.

"Yes let's get on with it guys. We still have time!" - exclaimed Olivia

The young rabbits had found an empty canoe on the bank of the river. It looked like it had been there for a while but just left with one paddle. As the eldest, Rico quickly went in the boat and managed to get his friends in too. They got on the boat and paddled down the river.

"I hope we don't see any alligators; I wouldn't want to be their meal for the day," said Woodie.

"We will be okay Woodie, don't worry" Olivia comforted him.

Ralphie was so determined and ready to do anything to accomplish his mission.

Suddenly,

the map slipped OUT

of Ralphie's hands and fell into the water. Without a map to guide the little rabbits, instead of going north, they went south which was a bad idea. The further they paddled, the more the boat was rocked by the river and Rico's paddle snapped after hitting a rock in the river.

"Look out!" called Rico

"We're going to get wet"

The boat went through the waterfall.

"Oh help, said Olivia, I don't like getting wet."

"Think of the alligators,"

"It's better than being eaten. What are we going to do guys; we are in the middle of nowhere. It is so dark.

How are we going to find our way home Ralphie?

I am really scared." said Woodie.

The little rabbits were all looking at Rico as he couldn't manage to paddle down the river. Woodie was really scared at this moment.

"I don't know guys, I was so determined to find the bottle of milk. I guess my dream was just not real. We should have listened to Woodie," said Worried Ralphie.

The little rabbits were very frightened...

Remember

"Children are a bundle of joy, fun, mischief, cute and interesting characters."

ABOUT THE AUTHOR

Kudzai Pasirayi is an ingenious writer who lives in Middlesbrough in the North of England. She enjoys teaching and spending time with Children. In her early twenties, she writes articles and books for children and adult interests.

"Ralphie & The Lost Bottle of Milk" is the first one on the action and adventure packed series followed by the second book "On A Wild Adventure". Watch out for the up-coming series Mischievous Ralphie in Action with his friends Rico, Woodie and Olivia.

www.mischievousralphieinaction.co.uk

Printed in Poland
by Amazon Fulfillment
Poland Sp. z o.o., Wrocław